BIG SISTER, Little Sister

BY
LeUyen Pham

Hyperion Books for Children
New York

Printed in Singapore
First Edition
1 3 5 7 9 10 8 6 4 2
Designed by LeUyen Pham
The artwork was created with a Japanese brush pen and
ink, and the color was produced digitally.
This book is set in Journal.
Reinforced binding
ISBN 0-7868-5182-1
Library of Congress Cataloging-in-Publication Data on file.
Visit www.hyperionbooksforchildren.com

For Big Sisters everywhere,
and for one in particular . . .

my Big Sister,
Lechi Pham

You were always the first
at everything,
and now you're my first book!

In this family,
we have
two sisters.

She's the Big Sister.

I'm the Little sister.

The Big Sister
usually does things first.

I'm the Little Sister.
I'm always
catching up.

The Big Sister gets all
the new clothes.

I'm the
Little sister.
I get all her
old clothes.

The Big Sister is very neat.

I'm the Little Sister.

I'm not.

The Big Sister
thinks she's always right.

I'm the little sister.

I know I'm right.

The Big Sister likes to try on lipstick
and act older.

I'm the Little Sister.
I can't wear lipstick
and I'll never be older.

The Big Sister
gets to stay up later
and watch TV.

I'm the Little Sister.

I go to bed at 7:30.

Sometimes.

The Big Sister
is good at a lot of things.

I'm the Little Sister.

I am, too!

The Big Sister
tells all the good stories!

I'm the Little Sister.

I get to listen!

The Big Sister
watches out for me.

I'm the Little sister.

I don't need to be watched out for . . .

most of the time.

My sister
is very good at being a
Big sister.

But I'll always be better than her
at being a Little sister!